MOUSE HOUSE

MOUSE HOUSE

BY RUMER GODDEN

Illustrated by Adrienne Adams

THE VIKING PRESS · NEW YORK

VIKING SEAFARER EDITION
ISSUED IN 1968 BY THE VIKING PRESS, INC.
625 MADISON AVENUE, NEW YORK, N.Y. 10022
DISTRIBUTED IN CANADA BY
THE MACMILLAN COMPANY OF CANADA LIMITED
LIBRARY OF CONGRESS CATALOG CARD NUMBER: 57-13962

PRINTED IN U.S.A.
SBN 670–05012–1
2   3   4   5   6   74   73   72   71   70

For

MARY GROVES,

because Mouse House belonged to her

Once upon a time there was a little mouse house. It was like a doll's house, but not for dolls, for mice.

Its walls were painted red, with lines for bricks. Its roof was gray, with painted tiles and a red chimney. The roof lifted up, and in the

house was a hall with a front door, a sitting room, and a bedroom, each with a window.

The wallpaper had a pattern of spots as small as pinheads, and the carpets were pink flannel. In the hall was a doormat cut from two inches of tweed. The sitting room had a painted fireplace, two chairs, and a table. In the bedroom was a tiny looking glass and a bed with bedclothes and a blue and white quilt. At the window were muslin curtains, and

on each sill stood thimble-sized pots of geraniums; the geraniums were made of scarlet
silk. On tin-tack pegs on the wall hung some
dusters no bigger than postage stamps.

Over the front door was a notice that said,
"MOUSE HOUSE."

Mouse House was given to a girl called
Mary as an Easter present. "It's to keep your
jewelry in," said her father, but Mary shook her
head.

[9]

"It's meant for mice," said Mary, and indeed
there were two mice there already, a he-mouse
in the sitting room and a she-mouse in the bedroom. They wore clothes; He-mouse had a suit
with a pale blue ribbon tie; She-mouse wore a
dress with a pale blue apron. They stood on their
hind legs, and their fur looked just like flannel,

their whiskers looked like bristles, and their eyes were as still as beads.

"Are you proper mice?" asked Mary. There was no answer, not so much as a squeak.

He-mouse and She-mouse stayed quite still, quite, quite still.

Mary was disappointed. "I thought mice ran," she said.

Most mice do. They scamper up and down the stairs and come into the larder and the cupboards and climb the table legs. They whisk into holes and run behind the wainscoting. The sound of their running can make a rustle and patter like rain, and they go so fast you can hardly believe you have seen them. That is how most mice run, but not He-mouse and She-mouse.

Mary waited for them to move—"Even a tail or a whisker," said Mary. Sometimes she lifted the roof up quietly to take a sudden peep, but they were always standing where she had left them; still, quite, quite still.

At last she took Mouse House upstairs and put it away on her chest-of-drawers.

"Don't you want to play with it?" asked her mother.

"Mice can't play," said Mary, but she was wrong.

Far down, below-stairs, in Mary's house, was a cellar where rubbish was kept, and there, behind an old broom in the corner, was another mouse house. It was not elegant like the one upstairs. It was a broken flowerpot made comfortable with hay. I cannot tell you how many mice lived in it because I was never quick enough to catch them, but it was brimful of mice.

"This overcrowding in houses is a terrible problem," Mary's father said as he read the newspaper. The mice in the flowerpot could have told him that.

When they were all in it asleep there were always some whiskers or a tail hanging out, an ear, a paw, or a little mouse leg. There was not an eighth of an inch to spare—if you want to know how small that is, look on a school ruler—and the youngest, a little girl mouse called Bonnie, ended up most nights pushed out on the cellar floor.

"She will catch cold," said Mother Mouse. "It's bad to lie out on the stone."

Father Mouse scolded the children. "Naughty!
Bad mice!" he said.

"They can't help it," said Mother Mouse.
"There are too many of them."

Then he scolded her. "You shouldn't have had
so many," he said.

But they were beautiful children. Their fur
was soft and brown, not at all like flannel; their
ears and tails were apple-blossom pink; and their

whiskers were fine, not like bristles. Their eyes
were black and busy, not still, like beads, and all
day those mouse children darted and scampered

and played. Mary would not have believed her
eyes if she had seen them. Even when they were
asleep they scrabbled and twitched as if they
were running in their dreams. "But I wish they
wouldn't," said Bonnie.

"Couldn't we move to a larger house?" she

asked. "Couldn't we find one? Couldn't we *look?*" asked Bonnie. But there was no time; with such a big family to feed, Father and Mother Mouse were gathering crumbs and bits of cheese and scraps of this and that from morning to night.

"A-t-*choo!*" sneezed Bonnie.

What games did the mice children play? Much the same as you: catch-as-catch-can and puss-in-the-corner—though puss was really frightening to them. They played I'm-on-Tom-Cat's-Ground-Picking-up-Gold-and-Silver, and blind-mouse-buff and hide-and-seek. Mary would have been surprised. An empty matchbox made them a cart, and for balls they had some dried peas.

"Come and play, Bonnie!" cried her brothers and sisters, but Bonnie had caught a cold and did not want to play. Two tears as small as dew-drops ran down her whiskers; mice do not have handkerchiefs, so that she could not wipe them away.

That night she found herself out on the floor again. "Mammy! Mammy!" squeaked Bonnie, but Mother Mouse was asleep, worn out with searching for crumbs and cheese.

"Mammy! Mammy!"

The cellar was cold and dark. From inside the flowerpot came soft snufflings and squealings, the sound of little mice happily asleep. Bonnie tried to get back, but she could not push in more than the tip of her nose.

"Where can I go?" squeaked Bonnie.

She wrapped herself round in her tail and curled up on the cellar floor, but it was too cold to sleep. She tried once more to push back into the flowerpot, but one of her brothers, dreaming of the cat, kicked her hard in the eye with his paw. "Ouch!" squeaked Bonnie, but no mouse heard.

"Nobody wants me," said poor Bonnie and began to creep away. "Where can I go?" she asked; there was no mouse to tell her.

She crept across the cellar floor until she came to a flight of steps. "Shall I go up them?" asked Bonnie. There seemed nowhere else to go.

At the top she rubbed her whiskers; she thought a strange light was shining. "Is it?" asked Bonnie, straining her whiskers to look.

The light was shining at the end of a long passage; it came from under the crack of a door.

A mouse can wriggle under a crack. Bonnie crept down the passage and under the crack and found herself in the hall.

The hall was filled with clear silver light. Bonnie blinked. She had not seen moonlight before. It was very pretty but very strange. It

turned her into a silver mouse, and that made her feel dizzy.

She crept out on the rug. She had never been here before—only behind the wainscot—and her whiskers trembled as she looked this way and that.

[25]

The grandfather clock in the corner went TOCK-TOCK-TOCK-TOCK, and Bonnie's heart, which was not much bigger than a watch, went *tick-tick-tick-tick-tick-tick*, far more quickly. Then it almost stopped.

The cat was asleep on a chair.

Bonnie had only heard about the cat; she had

never seen him; but she knew at once what he was.

W-H-I-S-K! I wish I could describe to you how quickly she was gone up the stairs.

Oh, how her legs ached and her breath hurt! It was like climbing a mountain far too fast.

"He's coming! He's coming!" squeaked Bonnie.

The cat had not moved an eyelid, but Bonnie was half dead with fright when she reached the top landing. "A hole! I need a hole!" she squeaked, but there was no time to look for one, and she wriggled under the crack of the nearest door—it was the door of Mary's room.

"I need somewhere high and safe. Another mountain!" And Bonnie ran up the highest thing she could see—it was the chest-of-drawers.

"Oh, my poor heart!" cried Bonnie; it was going *tick-tick-tick-tick-tick, tick-tick-tick-tick-tick* faster than you can say it. Then, there in front of her, she saw Mouse House.

"It's a hole! It's a house!" cried Bonnie.

The front door was open, and she flicked inside.

For a long time she lay in the hall. Then, when she was sure she was really safe, she sniffed the doormat with her whiskers.

[28]

She looked into the sitting room. He-mouse was there.

"Hello," said Bonnie.

There was no answer.

She touched He-mouse with her whiskers—which is the mouse way of shaking hands—but he did not touch her back.

"It looks like a mouse, but it does not feel like a mouse nor smell like a mouse," said Bonnie.

She went into the bedroom. She-mouse was
there.

"Hello," said Bonnie.

There was no answer.

Bonnie touched She-mouse with her whiskers,
but She-mouse did not touch her back.

"It looks like a mouse, but it does not feel like
a mouse nor smell like a mouse," said Bonnie.

"Can't you hear me?" Bonnie asked.

She-mouse did not say "Yes," and she did not say "No"; she said nothing at all.

"Pay attention," said Bonnie and flipped She-mouse with her tail.

She-mouse fell flat on her back on the floor.

Bonnie went back into the sitting room, where He-mouse had not moved.

"You had better lie down too," said Bonnie and flipped *him* with her tail.

He-mouse fell flat on his back on the floor.

That made Bonnie remember how much she wanted to lie down herself, not stiff and straight as they did, but curled up soft and warm. "Aaaahh!" She gave a yawn.

She tried to lie on the chairs, but they were too small. The table was too hard. She went into the bedroom and looked at herself in the glass, and the mouse in the glass gave a yawn too. "Poor little mouse. How sleepy you are!" said Bonnie. Then she turned and saw the bed.

She had not seen a bed before, but she knew at once what it was for. Whisk! Up she jumped and wriggled under the quilt. It is true that she put her tail on the pillow, but a very young mouse cannot be expected to know everything.

The bed was soft, the quilt was warm; in a minute Bonnie was fast asleep.

She was so tired that she slept a long, long
time. When she woke up in the morning, some-
one had shut the front door.

Have you ever been shut in? Then you will know how it feels. Bonnie ran round from room to room, round and round and round. She pressed her face against the windows until her whiskers hurt; she bruised her paws in beating on the door.

The table and chairs, the bed and the geraniums, were all knocked over; the looking glass came off the wall and the dusters were twitched

off their pegs. The wallpaper was scratched off
and the carpets were torn.

"Let me out! Let me out!" squeaked Bonnie,
but nobody heard. There was no one to hear.
Mary had gone down to breakfast.

He-mouse and She-mouse lay flat on the floor;
Bonnie ran over and over them, but they did not
protest.

"Mammy! Mammy!" squeaked Bonnie. "I
want to go home."

Far down below in the cellar Mother Mouse was squeaking.

"Be quiet and let me sleep," said Father Mouse, but she would not let him sleep.

"A mouse child is missing," she squeaked, and she shook him. "A mouse child is missing, is missing!"

"How do you know?" asked Father Mouse, and he tumbled slowly out of bed. He slept in the bottom of the flowerpot and got up last of all.

"I counted them," said Mother Mouse.

"*You* can't count," said Father Mouse. Neither

could he, but he did not tell her that. He watched the mice children hopping and skipping about. "They are all here," he said.

But Mother Mouse shook her whiskers. "There should be one more." She pulled all the hay out of the flowerpot; there were some bits of cheese rind, but no mouse child was there. She wept, but Father Mouse quickly ate up the cheese rind. It was his private store.

Upstairs in Mouse House Bonnie ran round and round.

When the flowerpot was empty, how dirty and small it looked. "How can anyone be expected to bring up children in *that?*" said Mother Mouse.

"What's the matter with it?" asked Father.

"It's dirty and shabby and broken and small," said Mother Mouse. "There's a hole in the bottom—a little mouse could fall straight through it or be cut on the jagged edges or fall out on the cellar floor. You must find me another house at once!" said Mother Mouse.

"What, *me?*" said Father Mouse. "I'm eating." And I am sorry to say that with his mouth full he said, "The houth ith for the children. Leth the children look."

The mouse children were delighted. "A new house? We'll find one!" they cried and ran squeaking all over the cellar floor.

They found an old coal scuttle, but it was full of soot. "We should be black mice," said Mother Mouse.

They found a flour bin with a hole in it, but all

the flour had not run out. "We should be white mice," said Mother Mouse.

A riding boot looked cosy, but: "What a long long passage," said Mother Mouse. "And it's dark. It needs a window at the other end."

There was no more room in a kettle than in the flowerpot, and a dustpan was not the right shape.

"It's too difficult to find a house," said the mouse children. They lay down in the hay and went to sleep. Father Mouse slept too, but Mother Mouse sat up. She wanted a new house and she was missing her baby. Every now and again a mouse tear slid to the end of her whiskers.

And upstairs in Mouse House poor Bonnie ran round and round. "Let me out! Let me out!" she squeaked.

Every morning after breakfast Mary made her bed. This morning, when she came into the room, she heard a queer noise; it was rustlings and scratchings and thumps and squeaks. It seemed to come from Mouse House. Mary listened: squeaks and thumps and scratchings and rustlings, and it did come from Mouse House! "My mice are *playing!*" cried Mary.

She ran to lift up the roof and look . . . and nearly dropped it.

Quick as a flash, with a flip and a thud, Bonnie had jumped out. WHISK! She ran down the chest-of-drawers and out through the bedroom door. All Mary saw was a flash of whisker and tail.

"They've gone!" cried Mary, but when she turned over the mess in Mouse House, He-mouse and She-mouse were flat on the floor.

"Then was there *another* mouse?" asked Mary.

What a sight Mouse House was now! The curtains were down, the paper was in ribbons, and

the carpets were ripped. Chairs and bedclothes,
geraniums and dusters were all mixed up; the
legs had come off the table; the quilt was torn
to bits. "It's all spoiled," said Mary.

There was nothing to do with Mouse House
but to put it down in the cellar.

Bonnie took a long time to reach home. She ran into a hole in the wainscot on the landing and lost her way. All day she trotted up and down those wainscot passages. Once she came out into the hall and met the cat; then she got into the bathroom where a lady was washing in the basin. "A mouse! A mouse!" screamed the lady and threw a sponge. The sponge landed on the floor by Bonnie and made her soaking wet.

It was not until late that evening that a tired, cold, dirty, draggled little mouse put her whiskers out of another hole and found she was in the cellar. She was just going to run to the flowerpot, when what did she see?

She shook her whiskers once, twice, three times before she could believe her eyes. The flowerpot was gone, and where it had stood, under the old broom, was Mouse House.

But what a different Mouse House! It was full
of scufflings and squeakings; out of every window and even up the chimney peeped little mice.

[54]

Father Mouse was in the hall, and on the door-step Mother Mouse was looking anxiously this way and that.

"Mammy! Mammy!" squeaked Bonnie.

"I *knew* there was one more!" said Mother Mouse.

For the mice, Mouse House was not spoiled at all; they found it far more convenient without curtains and a table and chairs.

They used one room for sleeping in, the other as a pantry. "That's better," said Mother Mouse. "It *is* better not to have cheese rind in the beds.'

Father Mouse hid a little under the doormat in
the hall.

The scraps of wallpaper and carpet and bedclothes made a comfortable nest; the girl mice
wrapped each of the geraniums in a duster and
used them for dolls.

What happened to He-mouse and She-mouse?
Mary had lifted them out of the house at once
but they did not seem to notice when it was
taken away, or that He-mouse's tie was off and

She-mouse's apron torn. "And it wasn't *you*
playing," said Mary.

She tidied them up and sewed them on a pin-
cushion and gave it to her aunt for Christmas.

The mice are very happy, particularly Bonnie.
She was a little nervous at first of being shut
into Mouse House, but the door soon came off its
hinges, with the mouse traffic going in and out.
When her brothers and sisters heard her story
they voted she should sleep in the bed. "So that
she can never be pushed out again," said Mother
Mouse.

"But if I hadn't been pushed out," said wise
little Bonnie, "we shouldn't have Mouse House."

How do I know all this? Well, one day, not a long time after, Mary hid in the cellar when *she* played hide-and-seek. As she sat there, quite quiet, the mice children came hopping out; hopping and skipping and scampering and jumping. "Then mice *do* play," said Mary.

After that she would often steal down to watch and listen and look.

"They are *my* mice," said Mary. "I gave them
Mouse House."

Then she stopped and thought, Or did one
little mouse come and fetch it?

When she had thought that, I think she could
guess the rest, and that is how she came to tell
me, and I to tell you, the story of Mouse
House.